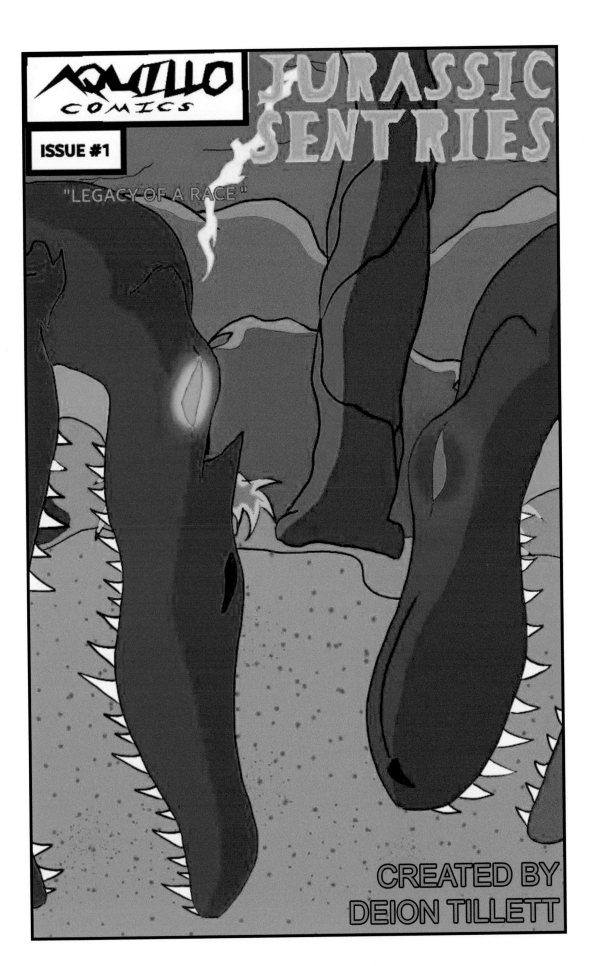

To order additional copies of this book, contact:
Xlibris
844-714-8691
www.Xlibris.com
Orders@Xlibris.com

ISBN: Softcover   978-1-6641-8688-0
        EBook   978-1-6641-8687-3

Print information available on the last page

Rev. date: 07/23/2021

Planet Saurna, a once peaceful world of powerful prehistoric warriors. There were four nations that formed this world. Paleozoic nation of the insects, Permian nation of the sea creatures, Cenozoic nation of the mammals and the most powerful of them all, Mesozoic nation of the dinosaurs.

In the Mesozoic Nation, there was a team that guarded and protected the nations from threats, they were known as Jurassic Sentries. I am their leader, Tyran, a Tyrannosaurus and king of the Mesozoic.

We kept the nation at peace until one of my closest friends betrayed us. Spinus, a Spinosaurs, who thought that our way of living wasn't enough. He believed that only the strongest survive and those that are weak shall not have any chance. He formed his own injustice team called Cretaceous Conquers.

Since then, this small battle became an all out civil war. A war that lasted for five years. The Conquers were ruthless, thousands of lives lost from the chaos. But nothing compares to what they did three years into the war.

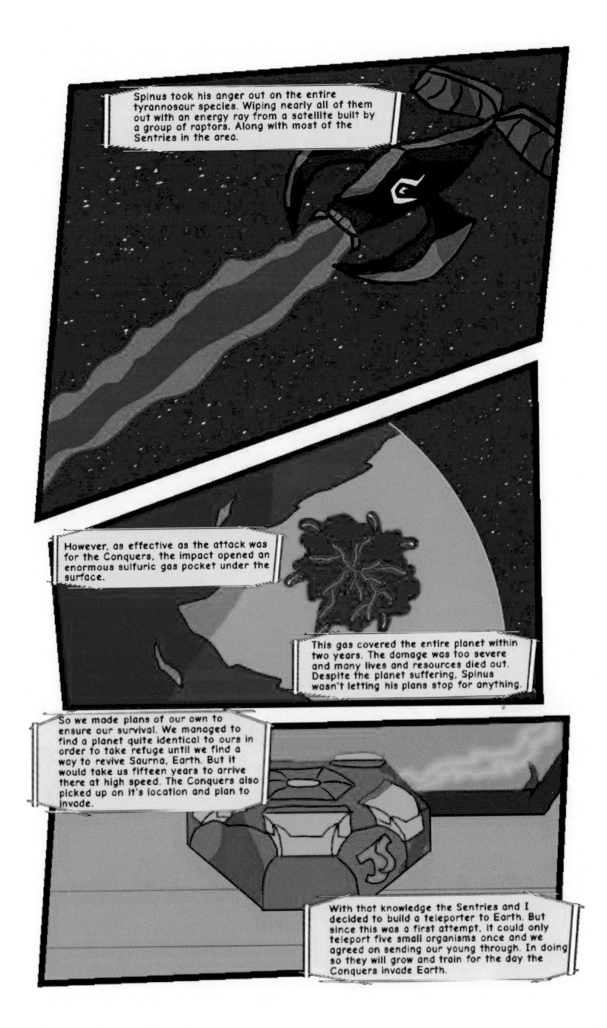

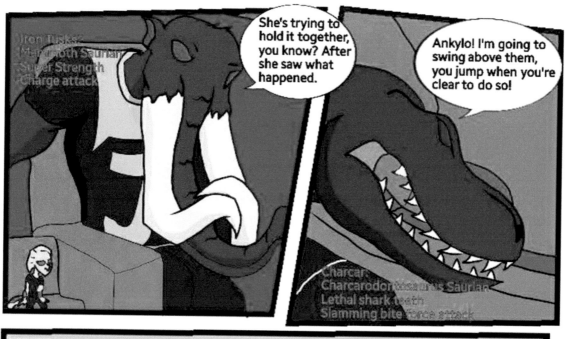

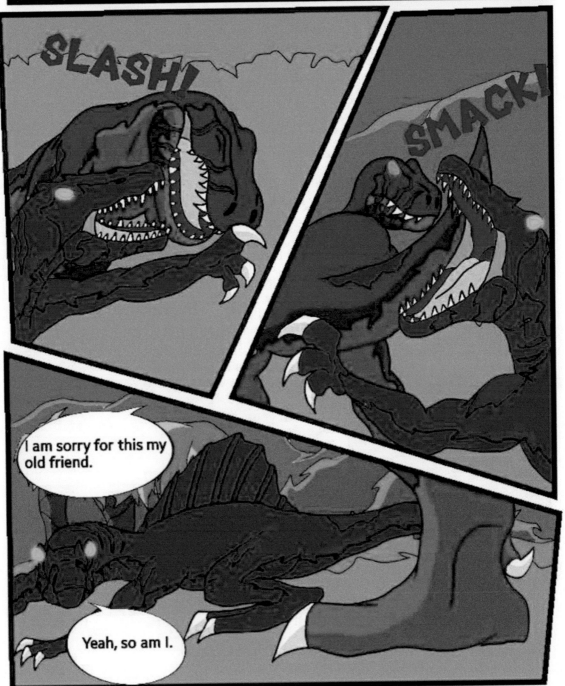

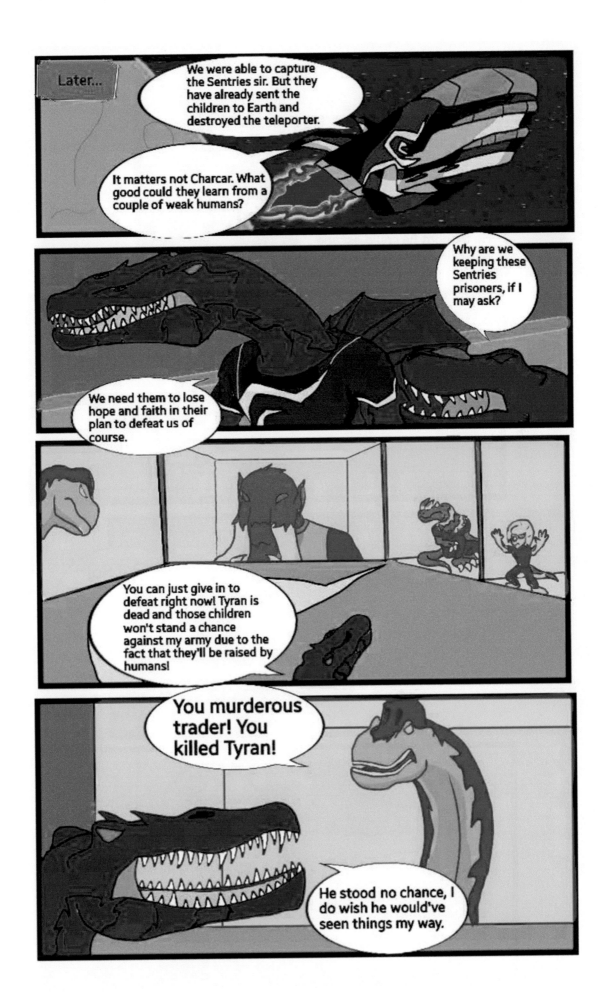

Seattle, Washington...

We've been watching you for some time now. We believe you are worthy to help us.

INDUSTRY OF SCIENTIFIC DISCOVERY AND RESEARCH

Ian Grimm:
Paleontologist
Genetic Engineer
Biochemist

So, Ian Grimm, Lexsis boltor, if you agree with my terms, then raise these five children as if they are your own.

Teach them about honor and compassion. Teach them to watch each other's backs.

Lexis Boltor:
Paleobilogist
Meteorologist

All of them, Rex, Spike, Don, AL, and Raptor. Teach them to become Jurassic Sentries.

Printed in the United States
by Baker & Taylor Publisher Services